A LITTLE
THANKFUL
SPOT

I am
thankful
for...

Written & Illustrated
by Diane Alber

To my children, Ryan and Anna

All inquiries about this book can be sent to the author at
info@dianealber.com
Published in the United States by Diane Alber Art LLC
For more information, or to book an event, visit our website:
ISBN 978-1-951287-21-4
www.dianealber.com
Paperback
Printed in China

This THANKFUL book belongs to:

_____

_____

_____

When you are THANKFUL, you are happy with what you have and experience, you don't compare yourself to others. When you write down all that you are THANKFUL for, it helps you focus on the positive things in your life. I'm going to share my list and maybe it will inspire you to create your OWN list! So, here it goes...
I am THANKFUL for...

Cozy SLIPPERS!

HATS! To keep my head warm!

SANDALS! To keep my feet cool!

RAIN BOOTS! So I can splash in puddles!

I am THANKFUL for...

UMBRELLAS!
So I can enjoy the rain without getting wet!

SNOWMEN
in winter!

FLOWERS in spring!

Feeling ANGER so I can become passionate about a cause, or stand up for what's right!

Feeling ANXIETY to warn me if I am about to do something dangerous.

School SUPPLIES!

READING,
because it's great
to hear stories!

TIME, and the ability to be PATIENT.

A cardboard BOX!

And all the CREATIVE things I can do with it!

I am THANKFUL for...

TOOTHBRUSHES, so my teeth can get cleaned!

Nutritious FOOD!

PAPER, to make THANKFUL LISTS!

TISSUES, to help my nose when it has sniffles.

I am THANKFUL for...

I created this
list of questions to
help you too! I can't
wait to see
your THANKFUL list!

Name _____

1. What are you THANKFUL for that is RED?

_____

2. What are you THANKFUL for that makes you smile?

_____

3. What are you THANKFUL for that is soft?

_____

4. What are you THANKFUL for that is very BIG?

_____

5. What are you THANKFUL for that is very small?

_____

6. What person are you THANKFUL for?

_____

7. What animal are you THANKFUL for?

_____

8. What toy are you THANKFUL for?

_____

9. What do you think dogs are THANKFUL for?

_____

10. What book are you THANKFUL for?

_____

Made in the USA
Coppell, TX
28 May 2020